STAR WARS

THE ADVENTURES OF BB-8

Written by David Fentiman

Written and Edited by David Fentiman
Project Art Editor Owen Bennett
Pre-Production Producer Marc Staples
Senior Producer Alex Bell
Managing Editor Sadie Smith
Managing Art Editor Ron Stobbart
Art Director Lisa Lanzarini
Publisher Julie Ferris
Publishing Director Simon Beecroft

For Lucasfilm
Editorial Assistant Samantha Holland
Executive Editor Jonathan W. Rinzler
Image Archives Stacey Leong
Art Director Troy Alders
Story Group Leland Chee, Pablo Hidalgo and Rayne Roberts

First published in Great Britain in 2016 by
Dorling Kindersley Limited
80 Strand, London, WC2R 0RL
A Penguin Random House Company

10 9 8 7 6 5 4 3 2 1
001–280584–June/2016

A CIP catalogue record for this book is available from the British Library.

ISBN 978-0-24120-789-5

Printed and bound in China

A WORLD OF IDEAS:
SEE ALL THERE IS TO KNOW

www.dk.com
www.starwars.com

Contents

BB-8

The galaxy is full of droids. There are big ones, small ones, helpful ones and dangerous ones.

One of these droids is called BB-8. BB-8 is an astromech droid. Astromechs help starpilots fly their ships through space.

BB-8 belongs to Poe Dameron. Poe is the bravest pilot in the Resistance. The Resistance is a group that protects the galaxy from the evil First Order.

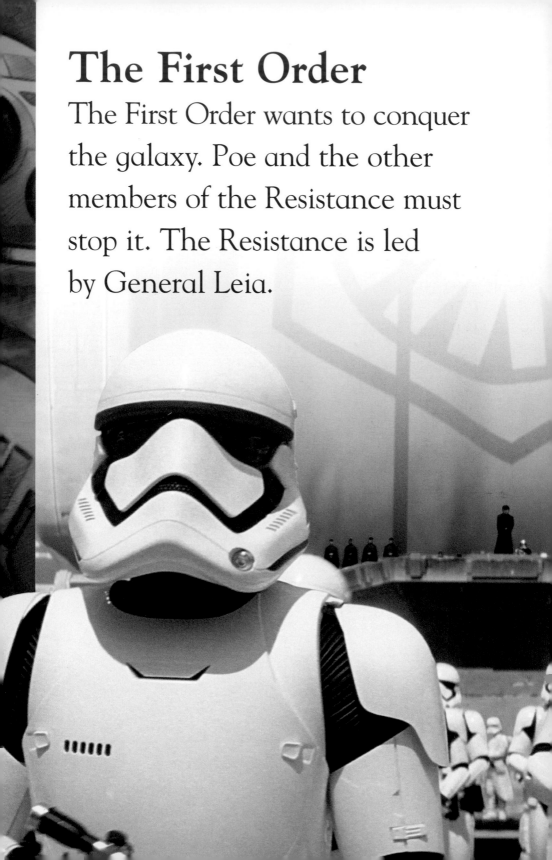

The First Order

The First Order wants to conquer the galaxy. Poe and the other members of the Resistance must stop it. The Resistance is led by General Leia.

Many years ago, Leia and her brother, Luke Skywalker, defeated the evil Galactic Empire. The members of the Empire who escaped became the First Order. Now the First Order wants revenge!

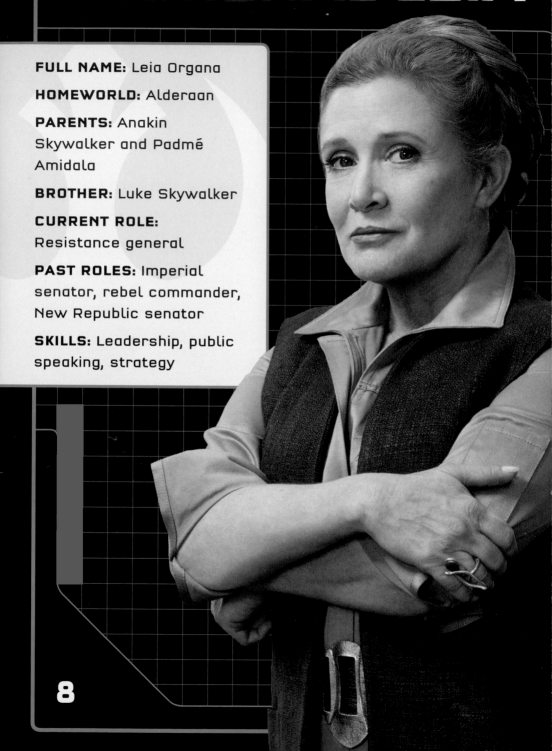

>GENERAL LEIA

FULL NAME: Leia Organa

HOMEWORLD: Alderaan

PARENTS: Anakin Skywalker and Padmé Amidala

BROTHER: Luke Skywalker

CURRENT ROLE: Resistance general

PAST ROLES: Imperial senator, rebel commander, New Republic senator

SKILLS: Leadership, public speaking, strategy

General Leia at the Resistance base

PROFILE:

- Leia fought bravely in the war against the Empire.

- She has now formed a new group to defend the galaxy from the First Order. This group is known as the Resistance.

- Leia's brother, Luke Skywalker, disappeared many years ago. Leia is trying to find him. She hopes that Luke will help her.

The village

BB-8 and Poe fly to the planet
Jakku to meet a man called
Lor San Tekka. Lor is an
explorer who has a map that
the Resistance needs. The map
shows where Luke Skywalker is.

Lor gives Poe the map, but then the First Order attacks Lor's village and takes Poe prisoner. Just before he is captured, Poe gives the map to BB-8. The brave little droid escapes into the desert.

In the desert

After Poe gets captured, BB-8 is left on his own. He is stuck in Jakku's hot desert, with no idea which way to go.

All BB-8 can do is roll towards the horizon, and hope to find someone who will help him.

BB-8 does not realise that he is being watched. A hungry creature called a nightwatcher worm is following him. Luckily, droids aren't very tasty, and it leaves him alone.

Meeting Rey

BB-8 is rolling through the
desert, trying to find help.
Suddenly he gets caught in
a net. A grouchy scavenger
called Teedo has grabbed him!

Teedo likes to take droids
apart to steal their technology.
Another scavenger called Rey
hears BB-8's frightened beeping,
and she rushes over to rescue him.
Rey agrees to take BB-8 to a
town called Niima Outpost.

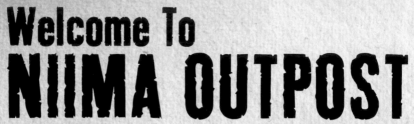

Welcome To
NIIMA OUTPOST

Niima can be a confusing place, so here is a guide for new arrivals.

Unkar Plutt

RULE NUMBER 1

Get scavenging. You will have to go into the Starship Graveyard and bring back technology to trade.

RULE NUMBER 2

Carry a blaster. Jakku is dangerous, with lots of hungry monsters and gangs of thieves. You will need to protect yourself.

RULE NUMBER 3

No fighting! Constable Zuvio will arrest anyone who makes trouble.

RULE NUMBER 4

Don't upset Unkar Plutt. Unkar is Niima's biggest, meanest junk boss. He has a gang of thugs that he sends after people who make him angry.

Constable Zuvio

Escape!

At Niima Outpost, BB-8 and Rey are chased by First Order stormtroopers. They run into an ex-stormtrooper called Finn. He is also being chased by the First Order.

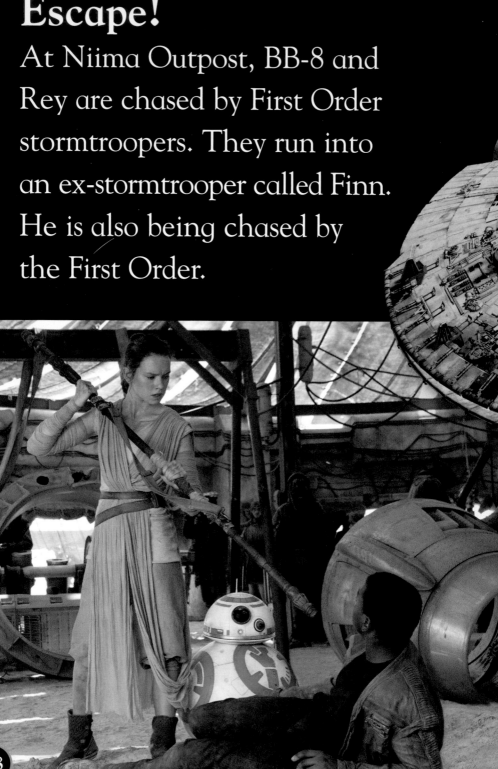

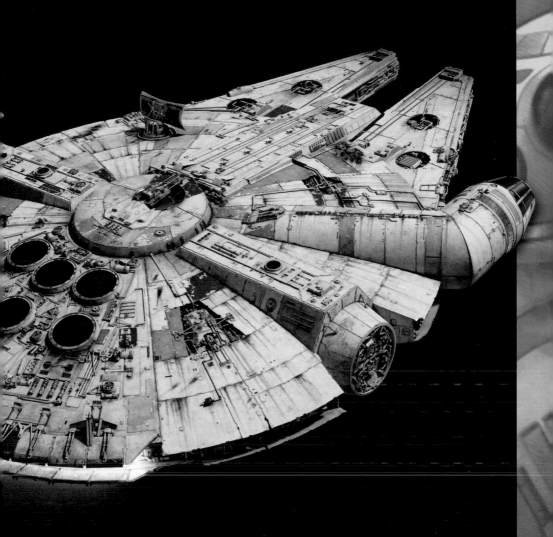

Together, BB-8, Rey and Finn
steal an old starship called the
Millennium Falcon, and escape
from Jakku. They get attacked by
First Order ships, but Finn shoots
the enemy down!

Han and Chewbacca

Just when Rey and Finn think they are safe, the *Millennium Falcon* breaks down! They are left floating helpless in space.

While Rey and Finn try to fix it, an enormous cargo ship appears. It swallows the *Millennium Falcon* whole!

The cargo ship belongs to Han Solo and Chewbacca. They are two legendary smugglers who used to own the *Millennium Falcon.*

Gangsters

BB-8 is nervous about Han and
Chewie, but it turns out they
are friendly. They are very happy
to have their old ship back.

Suddenly some gangsters board Han's cargo ship. They are enemies of Han and Chewie! The scary Guavians wear red, and the scruffy Kanjiklub wear black.

There is a big battle, but BB-8 and his friends manage to escape on the *Millennium Falcon*. Han takes a look at the map BB-8 is carrying. Half of it is missing!

Maz's castle

Han and Chewie think that they should get some help. They take BB-8, Finn and Rey to visit an old friend of theirs called Maz. Maz is a pirate who lives in a castle.

Maz's castle is very old.
It stands next to a lake on the
planet Takodana. The castle
is full of pirates and smugglers.
BB-8 has never seen so many
aliens in one place before.

BATTLE AT MAZ'S!

Rey and BB-8 are exploring Maz's castle. Rey finds herself being drawn towards the castle's dark basement.

Rey enters a mysterious room, and has a strong vision. She realises that she has strange powers. Rey is confused and runs out of the castle, into the forest. BB-8 follows after her.

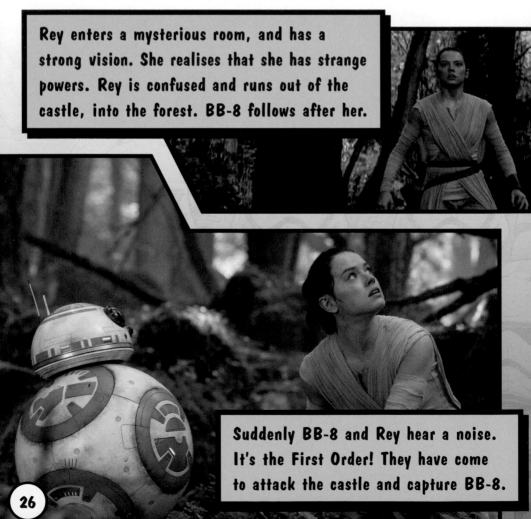

Suddenly BB-8 and Rey hear a noise. It's the First Order! They have come to attack the castle and capture BB-8.

The castle has been destroyed, and stormtroopers are everywhere. Finn, Han and Chewie try to fight back.

The Resistance has arrived! Its X-wings battle the First Order's TIE fighters.

Kylo Ren is the First Order's greatest warrior. He wears a mask and carries a lightsaber. Kylo attacks Rey in the forest and takes her prisoner.

The First Order retreats, and General Leia arrives in a transport. She meets with Han, Finn, Chewie and BB-8. They realise that Rey has been captured.

Battle plan

After the battle at Maz's castle, BB-8 and his friends travel to the Resistance base on the planet D'Qar.

Rey has been captured, and the First Order has revealed its powerful secret weapon. It is known as the Starkiller.

The Starkiller can destroy an entire star system. With this weapon, the First Order will be able to conquer the galaxy!

The Resistance has to destroy the Starkiller. The Resistance pilots put together a daring plan to attack it.

PILOT'S LOG:
JESS PAVA

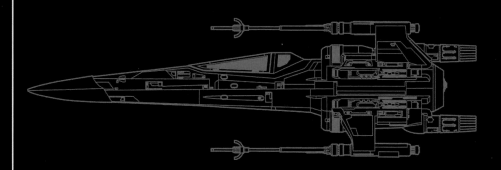

Blue and Red squadrons are going to attack the Starkiller. I'm not nervous. Our X-wings are faster and stronger than the First Order's TIE fighters.

☪ My code name will be
Blue Three. Commander
Poe is going to lead us,
and he always brings us victory.

☪ BB-8 has come
back to the
Resistance base.
I'm glad to see him.
I thought he had
been destroyed.

☪ I should get some sleep. It's
going to be a big day tomorrow!

Reunited with Poe

BB-8 hasn't seen Poe Dameron since Poe was captured on Jakku. The Resistance must have rescued him, and BB-8 is very happy to see Poe again.

BB-8 will fly in Poe's X-wing for the attack on the Starkiller.

BB-8 has been in many battles before, so he is not scared.

Poe is going to fly a special black and orange X-wing, called *Black One*. This is BB-8's favourite ship.

C-3PO and R2-D2

At the Resistance base, BB-8 meets two very famous droids, C-3PO and R2-D2. They both once belonged to Luke Skywalker, General Leia's brother.

C-3PO and R2-D2 helped Luke and Leia defeat the evil Empire.

fter the war, Luke disappeared nd R2-D2 went silent. R2 has een shut down ever since.

-3PO serves Leia as her assistant. le always talks to R2 even though l2 never talks back!

BB-8's friends

There are many droids serving with BB-8 in the Resistance. They each do different jobs, but they are all important.

NAME: PZ-4CO
CLASS: Communications droid (translates messages)

NAME: B-U4D
CLASS: Loading droid (maintains X-wing fighters)

NAME: M9-G8
CLASS: Astromech droid (helps starship pilots)

NAME: GA-97
CLASS: Spy droid (keeps watch for the First Order)

NAME: 4B-EG-6
CLASS: Power droid (a big walking battery)

Attacking the Starkiller

The Resistance pilots fly
to attack the Starkiller.
BB-8 joins Poe in his special
X-wing starfighter.

Rey manages to escape
from her cell, and she meets up
with Han, Chewie and Finn.
They attack the Starkiller on
the ground, while Poe and his
pilots battle the First Order's
TIE fighters.

BB-8 is very brave. After a hard
battle, the Resistance finally
manages to destroy the Starkiller.

Poe and BB-8 fly back to the
Resistance base. BB-8 is happy
to still be in once piece!

Victory!

Back at the Resistance base, everyone is happy that the Starkiller has been destroyed. It was a tough battle, and some of the Resistance did not return. Finn was wounded, but Rey rescued him.

R2-D2 wakes up, and realises that he has the missing half of BB-8's map. They put the map back together. Now they know where Luke is! Rey is going to find him. Everyone watches as she takes off in the *Millennium Falcon*.

Quiz

1. What kind of droid is BB-8?

2. Who does BB-8 belong to?

3. Who does Rey rescue BB-8 from?

4. What planet is Maz's castle on?

5. What is the name of Poe's special X-wing?

6. What is the First Order's secret weapon?

7. What is Jess Pava's code name?

8. Which droid serves as Leia's assistant?

9. Who has the missing half of BB-8's map?

Answers on page 48

Glossary

Blaster
A weapon that fires
glowing bolts of energy

Conquer
To take control of
something using force

Droid
A robot

Empire
An evil group that once
ruled the galaxy, but
which was destroyed

Explorer
Someone who travels
to places that no one
has been to before

First Order
A new army formed
by the survivors of
the Empire

Leadership
The ability to lead
people well

Mysterious
Strange, or hard
to explain

Nervous
To feel worried or scared

Resistance
A group created to
protect the galaxy
from the First Order

Retreat
To escape from a battle
or situation

Reunited
When things that were
once together, but then
separated, are put back
together again

Scavenger
Someone who
searches through
worthless junk
to find useful
things

Senator
A member of a senate
(a type of government)

Smuggler
Someone who
transports illegal goods

Starkiller
A giant secret weapon
built on an icy planet
by the First Order

Technology
Equipment made using
scientific knowledge

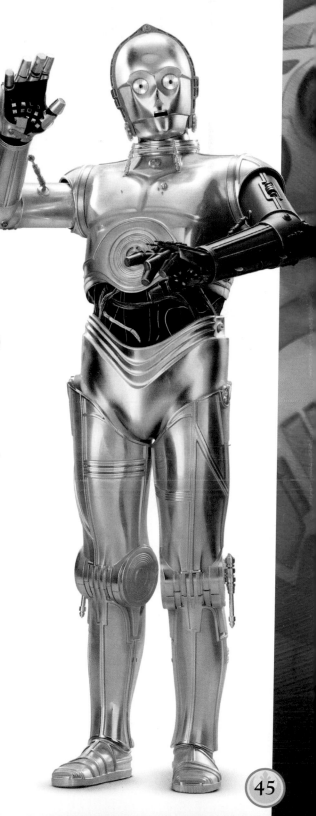

Guide for Parents

This book is part of an exciting four-level reading series for children, developing the habit of reading widely for both pleasure and information. These chapter books have a compelling main narrative to suit your child's reading ability. Each book is designed to develop your child's reading skills, fluency, grammar awareness and comprehension in order to build confidence and engagement when reading.

Ready for a *Level 2* book

YOUR CHILD SHOULD

- be using phonics, including consonant blends, such as bl, gl and sm, to read unfamiliar words; and common word endings, such as plurals, ing, ed and ly.
- be pausing briefly at commas, and for longer at full stops; and altering his or her expression to respond to question, exclamation and speech marks.

A valuable and shared reading experience

For many children, reading requires much effort, but adult participation can make this both fun and easier. So here are a few tips on how to use this book with your child.

TIP 1 **Check out the contents together before your child begins:**

- read the text about the book on the back cover.
- flip through the book and stop to chat about the contents page together to heighten your child's interest and expectation.
- make use of unfamiliar or difficult words on the page in a brief discussion.
- chat about the nonfiction reading features used in the book, such as headings, captions, lists or charts.

TIP 2 Support your child as he/she reads the story pages:

- give the book to your child to read and turn the pages.

- where necessary, encourage your child to break a word into syllables, sound out each one and then flow the syllables together. Ask him/her to reread the sentence to check the meaning.

- when there's a question mark or an exclamation mark, encourage your child to vary his/her voice as he/she reads the sentence. Demonstrate how to do this if it is helpful.

TIP 3 Chat at the end of each page:

- ask questions about the text and the meaning of the words used. These help to develop comprehension skills and awareness of the language used.

A FEW ADDITIONAL TIPS

- Always encourage your child to try reading difficult words by themselves. Praise any self-corrections, for example, "I like the way you sounded out that word and then changed the way you said it, to make sense."

- Try to read together everyday. Reading little and often is best. These books are divided into manageable chapters for one reading session. However, after 10 minutes, only keep going if your child wants to read on.

- Read other books of different types to your child just for enjoyment and information.

Index

Answers to the quiz on pages 42 and 43:
1. astromech droid 2. Poe Dameron 3. Teedo 4. Takodana
5. *Black One* 6. the Starkiller 7. Blue Three 8. C-3PO 9. R2-D2